Tell the Truth, Tyler!

written by JoDee McConnaughhay
illustrated by Jackie Urbanovic

for Mom, who encouraged me to write
and for Keith McCaslin, who taught me how

08 07 06 05 04 03 02   9 8 7 6 5 4 3 2

ISBN 0-7847-1048-1

Standard
PUBLISHING
CINCINNATI, OHIO

Half an hour before supper, Dad put down his tools and stared hard at Tyler's face. "Did you eat chocolate cake?" he asked.

"No," said Tyler, blinking his eyes and biting his lip.
"Are you sure you didn't sneak a piece?" Dad asked.
Why does he keep asking? Tyler wondered.

Then Dad took Tyler to the hallway mirror. There Tyler saw two big brown eyebrows, two big brown blinking eyes, one set of chocolate-covered lips, and one chocolate-covered nose. Oops!!

"Now," Dad said, "did you eat chocolate cake when Mom told you to wait?"

Tyler looked at his feet. "Yes," he answered softly.

"Why didn't you tell me the truth?"
Dad asked, gently wiping the chocolate
from Tyler's nose.

"I was afraid to," Tyler said.

"You know," Dad said, "it's not always easy to tell the truth. But God says it's the right thing to do. The Bible says 'Stop telling lies. Tell each other the truth.' Even if it's hard to do, speak up and tell the truth."

"My teacher found gum on the floor, and wondered who had the gum before. I felt bad and didn't tell it was mine. Is that a lie?" Tyler asked.

"Saying you did it is hard to do, but NOT speaking up is lying, too. 'Stop telling lies. Tell each other the truth.' Even if you feel bad, speak up and tell the truth."

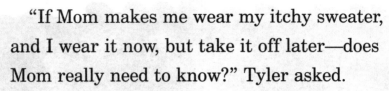

"If Mom makes me wear my itchy sweater, and I wear it now, but take it off later—does Mom really need to know?" Tyler asked.

"When you try to fool someone, this, too, is a lie, my son. 'Stop telling lies. Tell each other the truth.' Don't be sneaky, speak up and tell the truth."

"Last week I bragged that I had a new ball, but I knew it wasn't new at all. Did I lie or was that just pretending?" Tyler asked.

"If you pretend to have more than you do, it's a lie to let folks believe that it's true. 'Stop telling lies. Tell each other the truth.' Don't make things up, speak up and tell the truth."

"When I wash my hands at school, but don't use soap, which is the rule, is it a lie if I say I washed my hands?"

"Half-truths are still lies, you see—lies that hide the truth from you and me. 'Stop telling lies. Tell each other the truth.' Don't hide in a lie, speak up and tell the truth."

"I drew in a book the other day, but no one noticed when I put it away. I won't get in trouble if no one knows," Tyler said.

"A lie is a lie no matter what, even if you don't get caught. 'Stop telling lies. Tell each other the truth.' God sees the truth anyway, so speak up and tell the truth."

Just then, Tyler's little sister skipped
into the room. Dad stared hard at her
face. "Did you cut your hair?" he asked.

"No," Sarah said in a wee little voice.

Here we go again, Tyler thought, as he looked from Sarah's safety scissors to her crooked cut curls. And Tyler and Dad together said,

"'Stop telling lies. Tell each other the truth.' Even when it's hard to do, speak up and tell the truth!"

Suggestion to Parent

As your child becomes familiar with the story, encourage him or her to repeat the Scripture phrase with you each time it appears. Then, try letting your child *finish* the Scripture phrase each time it appears. Before long, your child will have memorized the verse!

"So you must stop telling lies. Tell each other the truth."
—Ephesians 4:25